To Francesca and Charlotte
    —S.W.

Always Copycub

Copyright © 2001 by Frances Lincoln Limited

Text copyright © 2001 by Richard Edwards

Illustrations copyright © 2001 by Susan Winter

**Printed in Singapore. All rights reserved.**

ISBN 0-06-029691-7

Library of Congress catalog card number: 00-112323

www.harperchildrens.com

Originally published by Frances Lincoln Limited, 4 Torriano Mews,
Torriano Avenue, London NW5 2RZ England

# Always Copycub

*By* Richard Edwards
*Pictures by* Susan Winter

HarperCollins*Publishers*

Copycub was a young bear who loved playing games. His favorite game was hiding, but he could never think of a good enough place, and his mother always found him.

In the spring the bears woke up from their long winter's sleep.
Copycub's mother stretched. Copycub stretched.
Copycub's mother scratched. Copycub scratched.
Then Copycub crept to hide in a corner of the bear cave.

"Can't find me here!" he called. "Oh, yes, I can," said his mother. She tiptoed across the cave, reached into the shadows, and lifted the small bear high above her head. "Got you, little Copycub!"

When summer came to the north woods, the bears spent all day outside in the sunshine.

"Can't find me here!" called Copycub, hiding in the bushes.

"Oh, yes, I can," replied his mother. And she lolloped through the trees, running straight to the young bear's hiding place.

"Got you again!" she said, kissing him on the nose.

In autumn all the bears gathered at the big river to fish for salmon.
"Can't find me here!" called Copycub, hiding behind the sticks
of a beaver dam.
But his mother splashed through the water and scooped him up.
"Oh, yes, I can, my little furry fish!"

One afternoon, while the two bears were exploring deep in the woods, Copycub thought of a really good place to hide. When his mother wasn't looking, he slipped away, ran down to a stream, and climbed the hill on the other side until he came to a hollow tree. With a squeeze and a wriggle, he pushed inside.

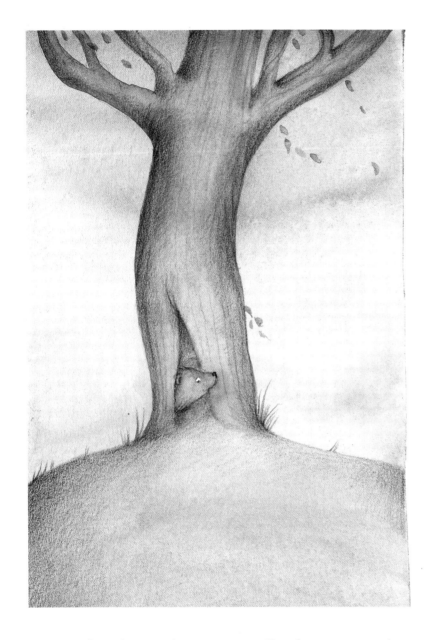

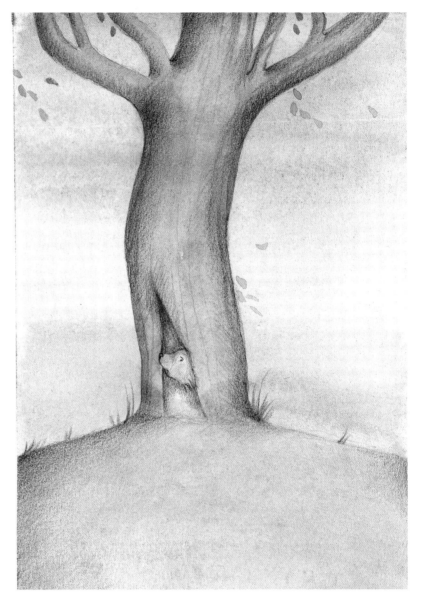

"Can't find me here!" called Copycub. There was no reply.

"Can't find me here!" he called again, a little louder. Again there was no reply.

"Can't find me here!" he shouted at the top of his voice.
But the only answer was the swish of the wind through the treetops.

Copycub felt very alone. He squeezed out of the hollow tree and began to run back the way he had come.

But he took the wrong path and was soon completely lost
in the darkening woods. He ran this way. He ran that way.
He didn't know what to do.

Copycub sat down and shivered.
Night was falling. An owl hooted,
and the woods made noises.
A leaf fell. A tree groaned in the wind.

Then Copycub heard a louder noise: a slow and heavy rustling
coming steadily towards him. He crawled behind a fallen log and
hid, making himself as small as he could and covering his eyes
with his paws.

"Can't find me here!" he whispered.

"Oh, yes, I can."
It was his mother's voice. Copycub was so happy to see her!

He jumped up and ran
into her arms.
"I knew you'd find me,"
he said. "I knew
you would."

When they were back in the
bear cave, Copycub's mother
told him never to run off
on his own again.
"I won't," said Copycub.
"I promise." And he snuggled up
close to his mother's warm side.
He was very tired.

"But if I get lost, will you always come to find me?" he asked.

"Always," said his mother quietly.

"Always, always?"

"Always, always."

Copycub yawned.

"Always, always…?"

He meant to say it three times,
but after the second time
he fell asleep.

So his mother said it for him:

"Always, Copycub."